LOTTIE'S DREAM

LOTTIE'S DREAM

by Bonnie Pryor
illustrated by Mark Graham

Simon & Schuster Books for Young Readers
Published by Simon & Schuster
New York · London · Toronto · Sydney · Tokyo · Singapore

SIMON & SCHUSTER BOOKS FOR YOUNG READERS
Simon & Schuster Building, Rockefeller Center
1230 Avenue of the Americas, New York, New York 10020.
Text copyright © 1992 by Bonnie Pryor. Illustrations copyright © 1992 by Mark Graham.
All rights reserved including the right of reproduction in whole or in part in any form.
SIMON & SCHUSTER BOOKS FOR YOUNG READERS is a trademark of Simon & Schuster.
Designed by Lucille Chomowicz.
The text of this book is set in 15 Point Berkeley Oldstyle Medium.
The illustrations were done in oils.
Manufactured in the United States of America 10 9 8 7 6 5 4 3 2 1

Library of Congress Cataloging-in-Publication Data
Pryor, Bonnie. Lottie's dream / by Bonnie Pryor; illustrated by Mark Graham.   Summary: As a
young girl in Kentucky, Lottie dreams of the distant ocean, but she doesn't get to live there
until much later. [1. Seashore—Fiction.   2. Frontier and pioneer life—Fiction.]   I. Graham,
Mark, 1952-   ill.   II. Title.   PZ7.P94965Lo   1992   [E]—dc20   91-39657   CIP
ISBN 0-671-74774-6

To Suzanne, Tonya, Chrissy and Jenny
May all your dreams come true—BP

To Emily—MG

E ven though she lived on a small farm in Kentucky far
away from the ocean, Lottie knew exactly how it would be.
  At night she lay on her cot in the corner of the cabin that
she shared with her brother, Josh. Ma had pinned a faded
picture of the sea on the wall, and in her dreams Lottie felt
the tides wash grains of sand across her feet. She heard the
waves tumble and crash against the rocks, and she breathed
in the salty sea air.

In the morning she fed Rosie, the skinny brown cow, and went to the woods with old Pete, the hound dog, to gather berries for Ma.

Her brother, Josh, pulled her braids and laughed when she got angry and stomped her foot. But he made a tiny horse and cart for Miss Daisy, her doll.

One day Papa brought home a newspaper from town.
That night Ma and Papa talked long after Lottie went
to bed.

"There's better land far away," Ma told them the next
morning. "A place called Kansas."

Josh laughed and called her a baby, but Lottie felt sure that her dreams were coming true. So she helped load the chairs and a chest with their clothes into the wagon.

Pa tied Rosie behind the wagon. Old Pete ran along beside
it until his feet got sore and Pa let him ride inside.

The wagon was hot and bumpy, and Lottie's skin felt dry
and itchy from the dust. But in her dreams at night, she
heard the ocean thunder and smelled the salty air.

One night when they stopped, Indians came to their camp. Lottie had to hold on to her knees to keep them from shaking. One of the Indians had sad eyes, but when Lottie smiled, he smiled back.

When Ma and then Josh got sick, Lottie helped Papa drive the wagon. It made her arms ache until she wanted to cry; but she knew that Papa needed her, so she didn't complain.

Ma got better, and so did Josh; and at last they reached their new home.

"But where is the ocean?" Lottie asked.

Pa waved his hand over the prairie. "It's a sea of grass," he said.

The grass was taller than Lottie's head, and in the spring there were poppies and daisies; but the winter was so fierce that Papa had to tie a rope from the house to the barn so they wouldn't get lost in the snow.

Lottie still dreamed about the sea; but she worked and she played and she grew, and one day she fell in love.

His name was Ben, and he whistled while he worked, and his hands were gentle. His eyes were as blue as the sea in Ma's picture, and it was almost enough.

For her birthday one year, Ben took Lottie on a trip to Maine to see the ocean. They took long walks along the shore, and it was exactly as she knew it would be. Lottie wondered if heaven was colored in blue and gray and smelled like a fresh salty breeze. She fell asleep to the tune of pounding surf and knew she was home.

But Ben said the sea was noisy and wild, and besides, they had babies to feed—Sarah and Baby John—and a real home far away.

When they got home, Lottie folded up Ma's picture of the sea and put it away in a trunk. Now she dreamed of Sarah and Baby John and Ben, and she worked and played and grew older.

Sarah grew up and then John. They moved away and had homes of their own. Their children called Lottie "Grandma"; and when they visited, she made them cookies and showed them meadows where wild flowers grew. But when Ben died, Lottie sat in a chair feeling sorry and sad.

One day Lottie opened the trunk and found Ma's picture of the sea. It was older and more faded than ever, but she looked at it for a long time. That night she dreamed once again of waves tumbling and crashing and of smelling the salty air.

"You're too old," her friends said. "You'll be lonesome."

But Lottie just said, "Sometimes dreaming is not enough."

Lottie packed her things. She found a house with peeling paint and a shutter that banged in the wind. But when she saw the porch overlooking the sea, she knew it was home.

Now when her grandchildren come, she shows them how to wiggle their toes in the sand and rescue a starfish tossed up on the shore. And after they've gone, the waves tumble and crash, and the sun turns the spray into a rainbow mist.

And Lottie sits on her porch and smiles.

Holm	DATE	
I		